MARVEL STUDIOS

THOR

FROM ASGARD TO EARTH

Adapted by Elizabeth Rudnick

Based on the screenplay by Ashley Edward Miller & Zack Stentz and Don Payne

Story by J. Michael Straczynski and Mark Protosevich

MARVEL

NEW YORK

Published by Marvel Press, an imprint of Disney Publishing Worldwide. No part of this book may be reproduced or transmitted in any form or by any means, electronic or mechanical, including photocopying, recording, or by any information storage and retrieval system, without written permission from the publisher. For information address Marvel Press, 114 Fifth Avenue, New York, New York 10011-5690.

Printed in the United States of America

First Edition

1 3 5 7 9 10 8 6 4 2

J689-1817-1-11046

ISBN 978-1-4231-4310-9

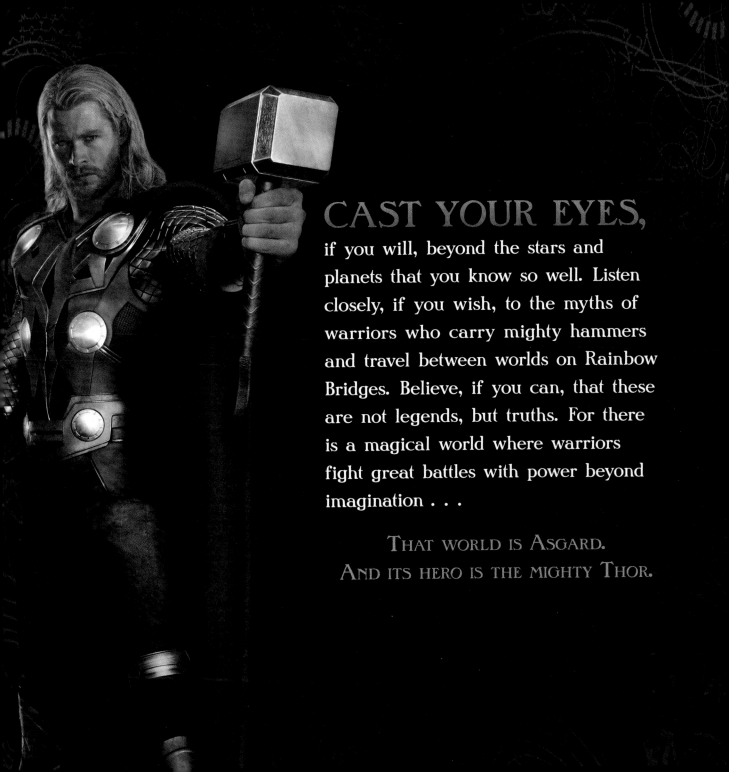

CAST YOUR EYES,

if you will, beyond the stars and planets that you know so well. Listen closely, if you wish, to the myths of warriors who carry mighty hammers and travel between worlds on Rainbow Bridges. Believe, if you can, that these are not legends, but truths. For there is a magical world where warriors fight great battles with power beyond imagination . . .

THAT WORLD IS ASGARD.
AND ITS HERO IS THE MIGHTY THOR.

THIS IS ASGARD.

Ruled by the majestic King Odin Allfather, Asgard is a world of great beauty, great power, and great peace. But that peace came at a high price, and the king knows it could be lost easily.

Odin's palace towers high above Asgard. It is here that the royal family resides.

A mighty ruler, Odin's throne is equally impressive. Made of the finest gold and shaped like his helmet, it sits in the middle of the throne room, demanding respect from all who enter.

Odin's rule has lasted thousands of years. During that time, he has acquired many items of great danger. These objects are kept deep in the heart of the palace, inside the vault—which is guarded at all times by the fearsome Destroyer.

The Casket of Ancient Winters is the most feared item inside the vault. Taken from the realm of Jotunheim by Odin to prevent the Frost Giants from taking over the Nine Realms, it has the power to cause instant and never-ending winter.

Sometimes lasting for a day, and sometimes for a week or a month, the Odinsleep is how the Allfather recharges the mystical Odinforce that gives him his powers. But during this time he is as weak as a mortal from Midgard.

Located in the palace, Odin prefers to be in this safe
chamber when the Odinsleep overtakes him

Beyond the walls that surround Asgard lies one of the most important places in all of the Nine Realms, Heimdall's Observatory. From inside the domed building, Heimdall controls the magical Bifrost.

The Bifrost, which is operated from the observatory at the end of the Rainbow Bridge, is how Asgardians travel between different Realms. It is also used by others to journey from Asgard to Earth.

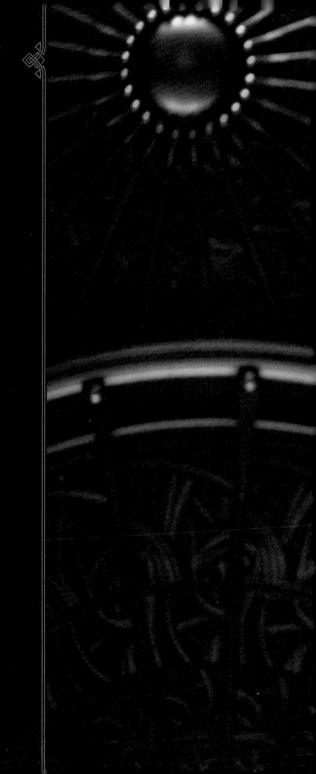

When the Bifrost opens and connects to another realm, it often leaves specific markings to indicate that someone—or *something*—has traveled between the realms.

Odin uses the Bifrost to banish Thor to Midgard. The Allfather also throws Thor's hammer Mjolnir into the Bifrost, causing it to also land on Midgard.

Whether on Asgard or Midgard, whosoever holds the hammer, if he is worthy, shall possess the power of Thor.

On Midgard, known to us as Earth, the Strategic Homeland Intervention, Enforcement and Logistics Division—otherwise known as S.H.I.E.L.D.—has detected these strange Bifrost ruins in New Mexico and has sent Special Agent Coulson to investigate.

Thor Odinson is now stranded on Earth, where he must live as a mortal. Here, in the New Mexico town of Puente Antiguo, stripped of his powers and his hammer, Thor must learn compassion if he ever hopes to return home to Asgard.

While in New Mexico, Thor encounters the beautiful astrophysicist Jane Foster, and her colleagues, the esteemed scientist Dr. Erik Selvig and college student Darcy Lewis.

In an attempt to show Thor what Earth is like, they take him to their lab and to the local diner. Soon, Thor comes to call them friends, and this small desert town his home.

But all is not well on Asgard. With King Odin in the Odinsleep, someone has sent the Destroyer to Earth to find Thor and make sure that he never returns to Asgard— even if it means destroying the entire town of Puente Antiguo.

But these are just some of Thor's amazing journeys from Asgard to Earth. Many think these stories are nothing but fantasy, yet you know better. And soon, a few more individuals will find out that these myths are very real.

AND VERY, VERY MIGHTY . . .